THERE'S A
DRAGON
IN MY
TOILET!

by TOM NICOLL

Illustrated by
SARAH HORNE

stripes tales

For my mom—T.N.

For Pops—S.H.

tiger tales

5 River Road, Suite 128, Wilton, CT 06897
Published in the United States 2020
Originally published in Great Britain 2017
by the Little Tiger Group
Text copyright © 2017 Tom Nicoll
Illustrations copyright © 2017 Sarah Horne
ISBN-13: 978-1-68010-455-4
ISBN-10: 1-68010-455-1
Printed in the USA
STP/4800/0362/0420

10 9 8 7 6 5 4 3 2

For more insight and activities, visit us at www.tigertalesbooks.com

Contents

CHAPTER 1
PAN THE PARTY PLANNER

"Echo-Romeo-India-Charlie, I have eyes on the objective. The chickens are in the henhouse. I repeat, the chickens are in the henhouse."

I looked blankly at the walkie-talkie in my hand. We didn't have a henhouse. Or chickens. I clicked the button to talk. "Pan, what are you talking about?" I asked.

Even above the noise of all the people gathered behind me in my living room, I could hear Pan sighing on the other end. "It's code, Eric," he said. "Honestly, are

Mini-Dragons the only ones who know how to use walkie-talkies correctly?"

"No, but not everyone gets to hang around the house all day learning stuff from old cop movies," I said.

"Fine. The message is: your parents are here," he said. "And now that I've finished being the lookout, can I come downstairs?"

"In a couple of minutes," I said. "Come down once they're inside. I'll meet you in the hall, and then you can hide in my pocket."

"Ah, the glamorous life of a Mini-Dragon," said Pan.

I turned to face the room. "All right, everyone, it's time!" I shouted before switching off the lights.

There was silence, followed by the sound of the front door opening, footsteps walking through the hall, the opening of the door, the clicking of the light switch, and then:

"SURPRISE!!"

"Ahhhhhhhhhh!!!" screamed Mom.

"Ahhhhhhhhhh!!!" screamed Dad.

"Mom, Dad, relax! It's okay!" I said.

"Eric?" said Mom, her fright turning to confusion. "What is all this?"

I glanced back at the dozens of people in our living room wearing party hats, the balloons scattered everywhere, the brightly-colored gift boxes piled in a corner, and the huge "Happy Anniversary" banner draped from the ceiling.

I thought it was kind of obvious.

"It's a surprise party," I said.

"Oh, right," said Mom, nodding slowly. "For whom?"

I slapped my forehead. "For you and Dad, of course. Happy 20th wedding anniversary!"

"HAPPY ANNIVERSARY!" bellowed everyone behind me.

My parents stared at each other in shock.

"Well," said Dad. "It's certainly a surprise."

"You have Eric to thank for that," said Aunt Ruth, appearing next to me. She had been taking care of us while Mom and Dad were out. "Organized the whole thing himself."

My parents' heads turned sharply back toward me. They looked even more surprised than before.

"This was all you?" asked Dad, unable to hide the doubt in his voice.

He was right to be doubtful, of course. I hadn't organized this by myself. In fact, I'd hardly done any of it. I just happened to be good friends with a Mini-Dragon. And Mini-Dragons are excellent at party planning.

The whole idea had been Pan's to begin with. Once he'd found out that my parents' anniversary was coming up, he had been like a Mini-Dragon possessed. I think maybe he wanted to do something nice for them to try and make up for all the trouble he had caused since his arrival. Or maybe it was just because he had enjoyed my last birthday party so much. Now that was a good party, although hopefully this time we can avoid firing anyone into a tree on a rocket-powered scooter.

Pan's party planning had consisted of:

- Organizing the catering over the phone. I had quite a time convincing him to order anything other than prawn crackers, though.

- Making all the decorations, although he struggled with the balloons—accidentally blowing fire into them instead of air.

PAN THE PARTY PLANNER

- Making the guest list and sending out invitations to all my parents' friends and family. We had to sneak a look in Mom's journal for their addresses.

- Engineering an elaborate plot where he called up Dad and pretended to be a radio-show host claiming that he had won a free meal at a top restaurant in town. That restaurant was Panda Cottage, the Chinese restaurant that had once delivered Pan to my house inside a box of bean sprouts.

- Our friend Min was able to convince her parents, the owners of said restaurant, to cover the bill. This gave us plenty of time to get everything set up and also allowed Min to tip us off when my parents were leaving.

Of course, I could hardly tell my parents that a Mini-Dragon had arranged their party, so I smiled and nodded, taking all the credit.

"But ... how did you afford everything?" said Mom, looking panicked. "Tell me you haven't been using our credit cards!"

"I haven't been using your credit cards," I said, rolling my eyes.

"Of course he hasn't, Maya," said Aunt Ruth. "We all chipped in."

"Oh," said Mom. "Well ... I don't know what to say. Thank you, Eric. This is lovely."

I could see her eyes beginning to well up, and I knew what was coming next. She wrapped her arms around me, squeezing me to within an inch of my life, then planted a huge kiss on my face.

"Yeah, nice one, son," said Dad, punching me affectionately on the arm.

Suddenly, a flash of light almost blinded us.

"Pic-ture," said Posy, my two-and-a-half-year-old sister, wielding her new favorite toy—a kid's camera that Aunt Ruth had bought her.

She was obsessed with it, always popping up when you least expected it to take a photo. It was a bit of a nuisance, especially as I had to check it all the time in case she snapped Pan. Usually it was okay, because Mini-Dragons can freeze themselves if they sense danger, so mostly he just looked like a toy. But she was sneakier than you'd expect a toddler to be, and the camera also had a video mode, so I couldn't take any chances. On this occasion, however, I was more than happy to pose for Posy. She took one of me, Mom, and Dad, and then Aunt Ruth took one of the four of us.

Pictures out of the way, I left my parents to mingle with the rest of our friends and family. The Blooms, our next-door neighbors, had shown up, too. Mr. Bloom was like a bigger version of his son, Toby—the same curly hair, the same bright red cheeks, and the same appetite. Together they had taken the buffet table hostage, the pair of them busy stuffing their faces with prawn crackers (well, I had to let Pan order some, didn't I?). Mrs. Bloom stood next to them dressed in something my mom called a "Power Suit," which isn't nearly as exciting as it sounds. Unlike her family, Mrs. Bloom showed no interest in the buffet, or anything else for that matter, other than the phone she was tapping away on.

"Mini-Dragons sure know how to throw a party," said Jayden, appearing at my side with Min.

"Yeah … they … sure … do," she panted. "Sorry … biked … over … here … as quickly … as I … could … after your … parents left. Where is … Pan, anyway?"

"Surely you let him come?" said Jayden. "After he put in so much work?"

"Of course," I said. "As if I could stop him even if I wanted to. He was going to come down and hide in my pocket once my parents arrived. I'll go and get him."

I walked out to the hall, where we'd arranged to meet, but there was no sign of Pan.

"That's weird," I said, stepping back into the living room. "He's not there."

"Give him a shout," suggested Jayden, pointing toward my walkie-talkie.

"Good idea," I said, clicking the call button. "Pan. Are you coming? Pan?"

There was no reply.

The three of us looked at each other with the same anxious expression on our faces. I could tell we were all thinking the same thing. Pan wasn't the type of Mini-Dragon to take his time joining a party. To be honest, I don't know if there is a type of Mini-Dragon who likes to take their time, but Pan definitely isn't one of them.

It was time to start worrying.

"Where could he be?" asked Min.

I already knew the answer to that. Whenever Pan went missing, the same person was always involved.

"Where is he?" I said, storming up to Toby.

"Mmph?" said Toby, a chicken tender sticking out of his mouth.

"Eric!" bellowed Toby's dad. "Good to see you, son. Always a pleasure to see Toby's best pal. Isn't that right, Margery?"

Mrs. Bloom's eyes flickered from her phone screen to me for a second before she resumed her tapping.

"He's not my best pal," said Toby, visibly insulted by the idea. "Eric's like my nemesis."

Mr. Bloom laughed. "Ha. Listen to him, Eric. Nemesis, my foot! He's always going on about you. Tells us whenever you get something new and begs us to buy him the same thing. Between you and me, I think he looks up to you."

"Gah! Enough!" snapped Toby, his face bright red. Before his dad could speak again, Toby grabbed the tray of chicken tenders with one hand and me with the other and led me across the room.

"What do you want?" he asked, stuffing another chicken tender into his mouth.

"Now, Toby," I said. "That's no way to talk to your hero, is it?"

Toby shot me a fierce look. "Very funny, Crispo," he said.

"The Mini-Dragon," I said. "Where is he?"

Toby removed the chicken tender. "What, you mean the toy you never let me borrow even though I always promise to bring it back? How should I know?"

"Because whenever he goes missing, you're the one behind it," I said. I could feel the anger rising in my face.

"He?" said Toby. "I know it's realistic, with its talking and flame-farting, but you're talking about this toy like it's real. You're losing it, Crispo."

"Come on, Eric, let's go," said Min as she and Jayden came over and pulled me away.

"But he's got—" I began.

"I don't think he does," said Jayden. "Toby is a terrible liar. I think he's telling the truth."

"Hey!" protested Toby. "I'm a great liar, actually. Maybe I really do have your silly toy."

I looked at Toby carefully for a moment and then turned to Jayden. "Yeah, you're right. He doesn't have him."

"Yes, I do!" said Toby as we walked away.

"Where can he be, then?" I asked, ignoring Toby.

"Let's split up," said Min. "I'll check out in the street. Jayden, you look around the party and make sure he hasn't decided to mingle with the guests. Eric, you search the rest of the house."

I nodded and then left the others and went to check the kitchen first.

No luck. I was about to head upstairs when Patches, our oversized, over-pampered, over-evil cat wandered past me.

"Patches," I said suspiciously. "You haven't seen Pan, have you?"

Being a cat, Patches didn't reply. Instead,

she looked at me with total disdain, stuck
her nose in the air, and wandered off to the
kitchen. I knew Patches hated Pan—and had
once tried to eat him—but ever since almost
having her whiskers burned off, she seemed
to have lost interest.

Just to be sure, though, I quickly checked
the cupboard under the stairs where Pan
sometimes hid from her. Nothing.

I was starting to panic. I mean, it wasn't
like we could just put up a "Missing" poster:

MISSING

HAVE YOU SEEN THIS MINI-DRAGON?

REWARD: $5.00 (sorry, it's all I have left from
my allowance)

DESCRIPTION: Approximately 6 inches, scaly

COLOR: Green

EYES: Black

WINGS: Two

CLAWS: Sharp

TEETH: See "Claws"

EATS: prawn crackers, mountain goats,
dirty clothes

I opened my bedroom door and breathed a sigh of relief—Pan was curled up on my bed. But his walkie-talkie was lying on the floor, and he looked miserable.

"Pan … are you all right?" I asked.

He looked up as if he hadn't heard me come in. "Hi, Eric," he said quietly. "Yeah, I'm okay, just feeling a little run-down, that's all. I was on the way downstairs when I saw your parents and the rest of your family and suddenly … I don't know, I felt funny. Think I just need a good sleep."

"Oh," I said. "You're not coming to the party, then?"

"No," he said, closing his eyes. "Think I'll skip it, if it's all the same to you."

"Of course," I said. "Hope you feel better soon."

"I'm sure I wi—" said Pan, his voice trailing off as he fell asleep. I took out the small washcloth that Pan had been using as a blanket from my sock drawer and placed it over him.

I quietly left the room, meeting Min and Jayden in the hallway.

"You found him?" asked Min.

I nodded.

"Is he all right?" asked Jayden, looking concerned.

"Yeah," I said. "I think he's just a little tired from organizing everything. He'll be fine in the morning."

That's what I was trying to convince myself of, anyway.

CHAPTER 2
CRACKING THE DRAGON CODE

It was two days later, the first Monday of school vacation, and Min, Jayden, and I were back in my room, watching Pan. He was lying on my bed again, staring at the wall, the gloomiest expression filling his tiny dragon face.

Jayden waved his hand in front of Pan. No reaction.

"What's wrong with him?" whispered Min.

"I don't know," I said. "He's been like this since the party. He sleeps in his drawer all night and then spends all day on my bed. Sometimes he sleeps, but mostly he just lies there. Hardly says a word."

"He looks like you've told him he has to go and live with Toby," said Jayden.

"He hasn't even touched his food," noted Min, pointing at the two unopened bags of prawn crackers beside him.

Pan let out a yawn.

"Is he sick?" asked Jayden.

"I'm not sure," I said. "Maybe."

"Have you consulted the Encyclopaedia Dragonica?" asked Min.

I jumped up. "Min, you're a genius," I said.

Min shrugged. "Yeah, I get that a lot."

The Encyclopaedia Dragonica is the ultimate guide to all things dragon. It's full of amazing facts like:

Encyclopaedia Dragonica

- Dragons only come in six different colors: red, green, black, white, gold, and beige.

- Dragons are often thought to have majestic names like Zahira, Dracara, or Faaaarrraaa the Magnificent. But actually, one of the most common dragon names is Steve.

- No dragon has *ever* captured a princess and forced her to live in a tower. These stories were made up by scheming knights in the Middle Ages who were hoping to marry royalty.

- Contrary to popular belief, dragons are not particularly interested in gold. They don't buy that much, and when they do, they generally prefer to trade items or use credit cards.

Pulling the huge book out from under my bed, I began flipping through the pages.

"Dragon illnesses, ailments, and diseases," I said. "Okay, let's see. What are his symptoms?"

Min put her hand on Pan's head. "He feels a little warm," she said.

"I think that's normal," I said. "He does breathe fire, after all."

"He's looking a little green," noted Jayden.

"He's a green dragon," I said, rolling my eyes.

"More green, I mean," said Jayden. "Don't you think?"

"I'm not sure," I said, "but he's definitely tired and leff … leff… that thing where he moves like he's half asleep."

"Lethargic?" Min suggested.

"Yes, that's it," I said. "There must be something in here about lethargic dragons. Ah, here we go."

Encyclopaedia Dragonica

Dragons are solitary creatures. Spending too much time in the company of other dragons can exhaust them. They become lethargic, irritable, and generally unpleasant to be around. Most dragons go their whole life without making friends and limit their family contact to birthdays and Christmas, when they generally put little effort into gift ideas.

The exception to this is Mini-Dragons. Mini-Dragons are the most sociable of all the dragons, and family and friendship are the most important things in the world to them. While a dragon tires easily from too much companionship, Mini-Dragons tire from too little.

Jayden, Min, and I looked at each other.

"Well, it can't be that," said Jayden. "Pan has plenty of companionship. He has us, doesn't he? How much more companionship does he need?"

Min rolled her eyes. "Don't you get it?" she said. "Family and friendship."

"He's homesick," I said, lifting Pan up and placing him gently on my knee. "Is that it, Pan?"

My Mini-Dragon remained silent.

"Pan," I said.

"Pan," I said again.

"Pan."

"Pan."

"Pan."

"Pan."

"What?" said Pan at last.

"Pan," I said gently, relieved to hear him speak. "We're just wondering if the reason you're sad is because you're homesick."

Pan shook his head. "No way," he said in a dull voice. "Mini-Dragons are excellent at not being homesick."

"It would make sense if you were," I said. Pan's family lived in the mountains in China, and he hadn't seen them for months. "Maybe seeing my family at the party made you realize how much you miss your mom and dad."

Pan seemed to think this over. "Maybe a little," he admitted.

"Don't your parents have any way of contacting you?" asked Min.

"Well, yeah, but through my aunt and uncle," said Pan. "Only adult Mini-Dragons know how to use dragon codes."

Me, Jayden, and Min looked blankly at each other.

"Dragon codes?" I asked.

Pan nodded. "Every Mini-Dragon family has one. It's a way for Mini-Dragons all over the world to communicate with each other.

Each code is unique, but they all follow the same pattern—two parts separated by a curled-up Mini-Dragon."

"Do you know yours?" asked Jayden.

"Yes," said Pan. "I've seen it a few times. But it's not much use to me because, like I said, only adult Mini-Dragons know how to decipher them."

I reached for a notepad and the smallest pencil I could find. "Pan, do you think you could draw your dragon code for us anyway?"

Pan took the pencil from me, grasping it with both hands. It looked huge sandwiched between his two claws, and he struggled just to draw a straight line. Eventually he gave up, tossing the pencil away. He picked up the piece of paper, took a breath, and then blew out a small blast of fire. The three of us jumped back in fright. Pan held up the paper. Scorched onto it was the following:

Min, Jayden, and I stared at the page for what seemed like forever, our mouths hanging open.

"I told you," said Pan. "It's gibberish."

Jayden raised his eyebrows. "Who wants to tell him?" he said.

CHAPTER 3

DEAR MOM AND DAD...

"Pan, that's an e-mail address," I said.

"A what?" asked Pan.

Min put her hands over her eyes. "I don't get it," she said. "How can someone who knows so much possibly not know what an e-mail address is?"

"It's not that unusual," said Jayden. "My parents are exactly the same way."

"An e-mail address, Pan," I said. "You use it to send messages to people over the internet. Long—that's your family's last name."

Pan looked confused. "But … the dragon codes are ancient."

"He's right—no one uses e-mail anymore," said Min with a chuckle.

"But Dad used to go on a two-day trek to the nearest city to find a temple where he could use the dragon code," said Pan. "He always said that one day, when I was older, he would bring me along."

"Maybe by 'temple' he meant 'internet café,'" suggested Jayden.

"Look, there's one way to find out if it's a real address," I said. "Let's send a message."

Pan let out a little gasp. "Use the dragon code? But you're a … human!"

Shaking my head, I stood up and opened my bedroom door. "Mom!" I shouted. "Is it okay if we use the computer?"

"That's fine, Eric!" Mom shouted back. "But I'll need it in half an hour for my class."

Mom had been teaching yoga for years, but recently she had hit upon the idea of teaching classes online, live-streaming them to the entire world. She was making a fortune. I had even gotten a little boost in my allowance for helping her set it up.

We went through to the computer room, which is what I call our spare room. My dad calls it Command Central, because it's the room he uses to plot his tactics for the Kickers. Mom calls it the yoga room because.... Well, you can probably guess why. And if she could talk, Patches would probably call it her room, since it was where she spent most of her time. She was curled up in the desk chair, but as soon as she saw Pan, she was out of the room in a hurry.

"'Bye, Patches," said Pan, smiling for the first time in a long time.

I raised the lid of the laptop computer and

then clicked on the envelope icon. I logged into my e-mail account and began typing:

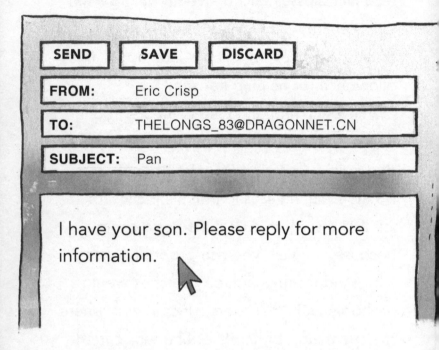

| SEND | SAVE | DISCARD |

FROM: Eric Crisp

TO: THELONGS_83@DRAGONNET.CN

SUBJECT: Pan

I have your son. Please reply for more information.

"What?" I said, noticing that the others were giving me funny looks.

"It reads like a ransom note," said Min.

"You write it, then," I said, frowning.

"Fine, I will," said Min, shoving me out

40

DEAR MOM AND DAD...

of the way. She deleted what I had written before cracking her knuckles and launching into her own e-mail.

SEND   **SAVE**   **DISCARD**

FROM: Eric Crisp

TO: THELONGS_83@DRAGONNET.CN

SUBJECT: Pan

Dear Mr. and Mrs. Long,
Hello! My name is Min, and I'm a friend of your son, Pan. I've heard so much about you both. Pan told us all about those horrible people knocking down your cave. Ridiculous! If I'd been around, I'd have given them a piece of my mind. Actually, I'd love to come over there. I'm Chinese, too, although I was born in England. The next time I'm over visiting relatives, we should definitely meet up. We could have lunch

"Min!" I said. "Get to the point!"

"Yeah," said Jayden. "You're writing an e-mail, not a book."

Min folded her arms. "I suppose you think you can do better?" she said.

"As a matter of fact, I do," said Jayden.

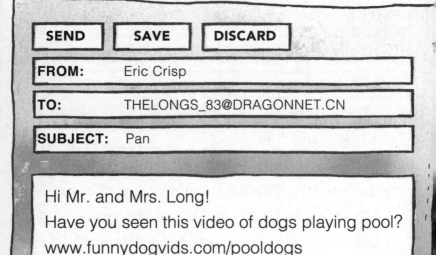

"Jayden!" I said.

"*What?*" protested Jayden. "It's an icebreaker, isn't it? It's a *really* funny video."

DEAR MOM AND DAD...

As the three of us argued about what to put in the e-mail, Pan jumped up onto the keyboard and began dancing across the keys, typing out his own message.

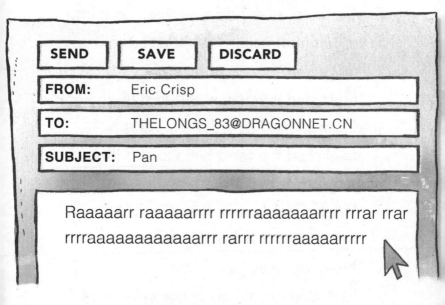

SEND	SAVE	DISCARD

FROM: Eric Crisp

TO: THELONGS_83@DRAGONNET.CN

SUBJECT: Pan

Raaaaarr raaaaarrrr rrrrrraaaaaaarrrr rrrar rrar rrrraaaaaaaaaaaarrr rarrr rrrrrraaaaarrrrr

There was an awkward silence as the three of us watched him type.

"Pan," I said softly. "I don't know how to put this...."

"Your e-mail is gibberish," said Min bluntly.

"No, it isn't," said Pan. "Mini-Dragons have our own language."

"Oh," I said. Pan hadn't mentioned this before. He had taught himself how to speak English before we had even met, so it had never been an issue. "What does your message say?"

"I just said it was me and that I was safe," said Pan. "And I asked them to reply."

He clicked the send button, and the message vanished.

"Well … that's that, then," I said.

"Now what?" asked Jayden.

"Now we wait," said Min.

"I still don't think this is going to work," said Pan. "I'm telling you—only *adult* Mini-Dragons know the secrets of dragon codes. We're just wasting our—"

PING.

DEAR MOM AND DAD...

The four of us looked at the monitor. A little mail icon was flashing in the bottom corner of the screen.

"What's that?" asked Pan.

"It's a reply," I said, clicking on the icon. A message opened up on the screen.

SEND	SAVE	DISCARD

FROM: THELONGS_83@DRAGONNET.CN

TO: Eric Crisp

SUBJECT: Pan

CLICK ME

"*Click me*?" I said.

"What does that mean?" asked Jayden.

"If I had to guess," said Min, "I think it means we should click on the link."

THERE'S A **DRAGON** IN MY **TOILET!**

"Well, obviously," said Jayden. "What I mean is, you don't just click on random links in e-mails, do you? What if you opened a virus? It could wipe out all the programs on your computer or steal all your information."

"Jayden's right," I said. "Mom would kill me if I downloaded a virus. I think we should take some time and think about this carefully."

Pan clicked on the link.

I sighed. "Or we could just do that."

A rotating hourglass appeared on the screen. Moments later, a light beamed out of the webcam, and then the four of us were staring back at ourselves from a little box in the corner of the screen. Then the hourglass vanished, and in its place was a bigger box. Inside it were two Mini-Dragons.

"RAAAAAAAAARRRRRR!" they cried.

"MOM! DAD!" cried Pan.

CHAPTER 4
CATCHING UP

"I'm so happy to see you guys," said Pan. "Oh … I mean … RARARRARRAAA."

The two Mini-Dragons looked at Pan with surprise. "You speak English?" said his mom. I could tell she was Pan's mom because of:

a) Her high-pitched voice

b) Her long eyelashes

c) Her sparkling red claw-manicure

d) Her lack of a beard

CATCHING UP

Pan's dad had a wispy white beard that was almost as big as him. He also wore a pair of tiny metal-framed glasses that made him look like a Mini-Dragon professor. "He's always been a clever boy. We should have known he would have picked up a language or two by now," he said, his face beaming with pride. Pan's parents both had the same hint of a Chinese accent that he did.

"I didn't know *you* spoke English," said Pan.

"Of course," said his mom, smiling fondly. "Your father and I learned to speak English when we went backpacking around Europe before you were born. Those were fun times. Oh, Pan, we were worried sick when your aunt and uncle told us you hadn't showed up in Mexico. We thought we might never—" She broke off mid-sentence as her eyes met mine for the first time. They flashed wild with fright before she let out an ear-piercing shriek.

"Pan! Behind you! Humans! **RUN!**" shouted Pan's dad.

"You touch my boy, so help me I'll find you and hunt you down!" roared Pan's mom, shaking her little fists at the screen.

"I'm warning you, we have a very particular set of skills," warned her husband.

50

"They involve lots of fire!"

"Mom, Dad, it's okay," said Pan. "These are my friends."

There was a brief moment of silence.

"Sorry, son," said his father. "There must be a problem with the connection. It sounded like you said these humans were your *friends*."

"That's right," said Pan. "It's a long story."

"It would have to be," said his mom. "Well, let's hear it."

Of course, they already knew how the story began—their family cave getting destroyed by builders. Pan's parents had planned to fly to the top of the mountains and settle there instead. But Pan hadn't gotten the hang of flying yet—to put it politely—so his parents had decided to send him to live with his aunt and uncle, bundling him into a container of bean sprouts on a ship bound for Mexico.

Now Pan filled them in on what had happened next, starting with the detour the boxes made when the restaurant that had ordered them went out of business. Then his arrival in the United States at Min's parents' Chinese restaurant, Panda Cottage, and finally Min herself delivering Pan to our house in a takeout box on that fateful Friday night.

Pan's mom let out little gasps at each part of the story. Pan wisely avoided mentioning the two occasions he'd been dragon-napped by Toby.

"Oh, dear," said Pan's dad, looking a little upset.

"It hadn't crossed my mind that the bean sprouts would have ended up somewhere else."

"It's not your fault," said Pan. "You couldn't know that Panda Cottage Mexico would give food poisoning to a bunch of pro wrestlers, forcing the owner to flee the country."

"I suppose that would be pretty difficult to predict," agreed Mr. Long.

"So these humans ... they're your ... friends?" asked Mrs. Long, smiling nervously.

Pan nodded enthusiastically.

"Wonderful," she replied in a voice that suggested she thought this was anything but. "What are their names?"

"This is Min and Jayden," said Pan.

"Nice to meet you," my friends chorused.

Pan's parents nodded and smiled politely.

"And this is Eric," said Pan, pointing

proudly at me. "He's been letting me sleep in his sock drawer."

"His sock drawer?" said Pan's mom, looking aghast.

Feeling a little awkward, I smiled and gave her a little wave.

"Don't be like that, Mom," said Pan. "It's the best bed I've ever had. Much comfier than sleeping on rocks like at home."

Her face softened a little. "Yes, well, I guess we must thank you, Eric, for taking care of our son," she said. "I hope he hasn't been any trouble."

I stared at the screen, trying to figure out how to answer that, then looked down at Pan, who was waving his hands and shaking his head furiously.

"Um..."

"Er..."

"Well..."

"No," I said, eventually. "No trouble at all."

"Well, I'm Mr. Long," said Pan's dad. "But you can call me Cheng. And this is my wife, Isabel—"

"And you can call me Mrs. Long," she said firmly before turning her attention back to Pan. "You look healthy enough. That's something, I suppose. How is the mountain goat in the United States, anyway? I've heard it's very bland over there."

Pan and I exchanged glances. "Actually, Mom, I haven't had that much goat recently. In fact, none at all."

Mrs. Long looked horrified. "But you're a Mini-Dragon," she said. "What else could you possibly be eating?"

"They have these things called prawn crackers," said Pan.

"Prawn crackers?" she repeated, covering

her mouth. "Jumping dragons, it's worse than I thought."

"Oh, I don't know," said Pan's dad. "I used to enjoy a good prawn cracker. They are one of the three Mini-Dragon food groups, after all."

His wife shot him a look. "Yes, and so is dirty laundry, if you believe everything you read. Would you have our son eating that, too?"

Pan's dad started to lick his snout. "Actually, I was always partial to a nice tea-stained vest as a boy. Or a good pair of muddy pants. I was even known to enjoy a tomato-juice-soaked sweater from time to time. Had to be in the mood for those, of course...."

"A growing Mini-Dragon should be eating mountain goat!" declared Pan's mom conclusively.

An awkward silence fell over the room. Min, Jayden, and I stared at our shoes.

"Um ... Mom, you look in great shape, by the way," said Pan.

His mother smiled and waved him away. "Oh, stop," she said.

"No, seriously," said Pan. "Have you been working out?"

"Well ... yes, I have," she said proudly. "There are these yoga classes I've been watching on the internet. It's the only thing that's helped with the stress I've been under since you went missing. The woman that does it is a bit ... *different* for my taste, but she's a very good teacher. In fact, I'll have to go soon, because her class starts in a few minutes."

The four of us looked at each other with stunned expressions. *Nah,* I thought, *it couldn't be.... Could it?*

"What's wrong?" asked Mrs. Long.

CATCHING UP

"Never mind," said Pan, squinting at the screen. I wondered what he was looking at, as all I could see in the background was a pile of rocks. "Wait ... are you guys in the mountains right now?" asked Pan. "How can you be on the internet?"

"It's our new neighbors," replied his father excitedly. "Say what you want about them, and believe me, your mother did, but the humans that knocked down our old cave and put up all those new buildings sure know a thing or two about Wi-Fi. We even get a strong signal all the way up here in our new cave. With the Mini-Generator and laptop computer I picked up, it means we don't have to keep going back and forth to internet cafés in the dead of night."

"Hang on ... you 'picked up' a Mini-Generator and a laptop? You just went into a store and bought them?" Pan asked.

His parents burst out laughing. "Oh, darling," said his mom. "Don't be so silly."

The little Mini-Dragon frowned. "So you stole them, then?"

The smiles on his parents' faces turned to shocked expressions. "Now, son," said Pan's dad, "how could you suggest such a thing? We made sure the owners received fair payment."

Pan let out a groan. "You left them a goat, didn't you?"

"A *delicious* goat," corrected Pan's dad.

Pan shook his head in disbelief.

"Anyway, we must be going now," said his mom. "Yoga calls."

Pan looked a little sad. "Can we talk again soon?" he asked.

"Of course, sweetheart," she replied. "We'll have plenty of time to catch up before Aunt Maria and Uncle Fernando arrive at Eric's house."

"Oh, that's good," said Pan.

A pause.

"Wait.... *What?*" said Pan. "Why are they coming here?"

"We're sending them to get you, of course," she said. "Pan, we've been so worried—we've sent messages to all the Mini-Dragon families around the world. We've had Mini-Dragons searching the continents for you. Your dad and I must have flown across most of China ourselves. And your aunt and uncle have traveled all the way to Spain looking for you."

Mr. Long made a little coughing noise. "Actually, dear, they're on vacation," he said.

Mrs. Long glared at her husband. "What? But they told me they had a tip— Oh, I should have known. Well, I suppose it doesn't matter now, I'll get them to pick you up on their way back to Mexico. Just let them even try getting out of it after lying to me."

Pan's face dropped. He looked even sadder than before. And this time I felt it, too—we all did. "But I don't want to live with them," he said. "They're horrible. I like it here, with Eric."

"Come on now, Pan," said Mrs. Long in a soft voice. "I'm sure you've had an exciting time with your new ... *friends*, and we're extremely grateful to them for taking care of you, but your place is with your family. With other Mini-Dragons."

"But Mom—" protested Pan.

"Butting's for goats," said his father. "Now be a good boy and e-mail us Eric's home address. Speak to you soon."

And with that, they were gone.

"Eric!" shouted Mom from downstairs. "Wrap it up."

"Okay!" I shouted, my voice breaking as I spoke.

The four of us returned to my room. We sat down on my bed, and no one spoke for a long time.

CHAPTER 5
WAITING

We spent a long time trying to come up with ways to keep Pan from having to leave. Here was what we had:

1. Trick Pan's aunt and uncle into taking Toby to Mexico instead of Pan. Not sure how this would work—maybe dress Toby up in a dragon costume? They might wonder about his weight, though—too many prawn crackers?

2. Run away? I didn't think my mom would agree to this. Min pointed out that we wouldn't actually be asking for permission. Then Pan asked how we would get all the stuff out of my room. Min just shook her head and told us to forget it.

3. Move Pan to Min or Jayden's house for a while. Neither Min nor Jayden seemed all that happy with this idea, even though I told them he's only actually destroyed my room once.

4. Send Pan to live with Toby—HAHAHA! No, come on, let's be serious here.

5. Convince Pan's parents to let him stay.

Number 5 seemed like our best shot, but the more Pan spoke to his parents, the better the Toby-in-a-dragon-costume idea seemed to get.

A few days later, Pan was in the computer room, speaking to his parents again. Min, Jayden, and I were watching, hoping that he could talk them into changing their minds.

"I'm sorry, Pan, but the answer is no," said Pan's mom. "A Mini-Dragon's place is with other dragons."

"But why those Mini-Dragons?" asked Pan. "They're bullies."

Mr. Long gave a little chuckle. "They're not bullies, they're ... well, they're...." He turned to his wife. "Help me out, Isabel."

"They're ... a bit stricter than we are," she agreed. "But that's not such a bad thing."

"Can't I at least come back home?" asked Pan.

"We've talked about this, son," said Mr. Long. "Our altitude is too dangerous for a Mini-Dragon that can't fly."

"Well, why don't you guys come and live here?" suggested Pan. "There's plenty of room."

"Umm … Pan … hang on a second…," I started, before Pan's mom interrupted.

"The Longs have lived in these mountains for thousands of years," she said. "It's our home."

"It was my home, too," whispered Pan, hanging his head.

Pan's mom nodded. "Yes, and once your aunt and uncle finish your education, you can come back to it. I've spoken to them and they should be with you soon, so you might want to stop wasting the time you have left with your friends by arguing with us."

Once the call ended, the four of us slunk back to my room, defeated.

"I don't want to go," said Pan. "All I wanted was to see my parents again, but now I'm going to lose my friends."

Min picked him up and gave him a kiss on the snout. "You'll always be our friend, Pan."

"Yeah," said Jayden. "We'll talk all the time online—now that you know what an e-mail address is, I'm sure we can get you into instant messaging, too."

The thought of being away from Pan was unbearable, but I didn't want to think about it anymore. "Your mom's right," I said, "about making the most of our time together. Let's do something other than moping around."

"Like what?" asked Pan, jumping out of Min's hand.

"We could play some games," suggested Jayden.

Pan shook his head. "Not in the mood."

"Why don't we go out?" said Min.

"Nah," said Pan.

"We need to do something, Pan," I said. "Who knows how much time we have left? Do you really want to spend it sitting here waiting for your aunt and uncle to show up?"

Pan looked up at me defiantly. "No," he said. "You're right—let's go out. Evergreen Park. I can ride the ducks again. Not the swans, though. They didn't seem to like it last time."

"Yeah!" I said, punching the air. "Let's go! Wait—what's wrong?"

Pan's face had gone a bit red. "Nothing. Just realized I need to use the little dragon's room. Back in a minute."

We waited as Pan headed off to the

bathroom. About a minute later, I heard his tiny voice yell, "Eric, I think you'd better get in here!"

I screwed up my face. "No, thanks!"

"Seriously, Eric, come here. Right now!"

I gave Min and Jayden a worried look and entered the bathroom, scared of what I might find. But all I saw was Pan standing on the edge of the toilet bowl, peering in.

"What is it?" I asked.

"Look," said Pan, pointing toward the water. Finally, I could see what he was talking about. The water inside the toilet was bubbling. Little bubbles at first, but then bigger and bigger until—

WWHHHOOOOOSSSHHH!

A jet of water exploded out of the toilet, sending us both flying backward.

And then there they were, walking toward us across the soaked bathroom floor. Two Mini-Dragons. Two miserable-looking Mini-Dragons in wetsuits, wearing little glass helmets on their heads.

They unzipped themselves, then tossed aside their diving equipment.

It was fairly obvious which one was which—Aunt Maria was the taller of the pair by a couple of inches. She quickly wrapped her head in an expensive-looking silk scarf before putting on a pair of dark glasses, both of which she pulled from a small plastic bag. Uncle Fernando, meanwhile, was the roundest looking Mini-Dragon I had seen so far. The only thing he wore was a grumpy expression and a brown waterproof backpack.

Pan and I looked at each other. Evergreen Park would have to wait.

CHAPTER 6

HELLO, GOOD-BYE

"So you're Erica, then?" said Uncle Fernando, a trace of a Spanish accent in his voice.
"They said we should speak English, since you haven't bothered to learn Mini-Dragon."

"Eric," I said. "Erica is a girl's name."

Uncle Fernando looked at me suspiciously. "You're a boy, are you?" he asked.

"Yes," I said, annoyed by his rudeness. In fact, I got the feeling he knew all this, but was just trying to rile me up for some reason.

The little round dragon gave a shrug.
"You humans all look the same to me."
"What's going on?" asked Min as she
and Jayden entered the bathroom behind us.

"Ugh, there's more of them," snapped Aunt Maria. "Pan Long, get away from those filthy humans right now. You don't know where they've been."

"*We're* filthy?" I said. "You two just came out of the toilet!"

"Of course we did," said Uncle Fernando. "Across the seas, it's a straight flight, but in the cities, the sewer network is the most efficient and safest way for a Mini-Dragon to travel. Every Mini-Dragon knows that."

"Pan, come here and give your aunt a kiss," said Aunt Maria.

A reluctant Pan had only taken a couple of steps toward her when she dragon-handled him into a hug and planted a smacker right on his snout. Under normal circumstances I might have had a good laugh, but somehow it didn't seem very funny right then.

"Let me get a good look at you," she

said, shoving Pan back. "Just as I thought—
you're skin and bones. You don't look any
bigger than when we saw you last year."

"That's because this human has had
him living off prawn crackers," said Uncle
Fernando.

"Actually, according to the *Encyclopaedia
Dragonica*, prawn crackers contain
everything a Mini-Dragon needs for a healthy
diet," I said. If anything, I was pretty sure
Pan had put on weight since I first met him. I
mean, he wasn't as well fed as his uncle, that
was for sure, but it's not like he was wasting
away, either.

Pan's relatives looked at each other with
stunned expressions.

"Maria," said Uncle Fernando, "maybe
I got some water in my ears back there …
or did that human just lecture us about the
dietary habits of Mini-Dragons?"

"Thinks he knows all about us because he read it in some book," said Aunt Maria.

"Know better than us, do you, boy?" shouted Uncle Fernando, puffing out his chest.

"No, no…," I said, taking a step backward and accidentally knocking over a bottle of shampoo and a Scuba Dave toy that had been resting on the edge of the bathtub.

Aunt Maria peered at me over her sunglasses. "A bit old for toys, aren't we?" she said.

"I'm nine," I said defensively.

"Exactly," she replied.

My face flushed red as I put the bottle and the toy back. I tried to think of a clever reply, but all I could manage was, "Get lost."

"How dare you speak to my wife like that!" said Uncle Fernando, holding up his tiny claws as fists.

Aunt Maria touched her husband's arm.

"Leave it, Fernando. He's not worth it."

Uncle Fernando nodded. "You're right, my love," he said, dropping his arms. "Typical human. I just can't stand them."

Pan, Min, Jayden, and I frowned in unison. "What's wrong with humans?" Min asked.

Aunt Maria put her head in her hands. "Oh, no," she groaned. "You had to ask. Now he's going to do the song."

Uncle Fernando spread his wings, flew up, and perched himself on the edge of the bathtub. "I'll tell you what's wrong with humans." He started to sing:

They're big and they're smelly,
With bellies like ... pudding.
They're mean and they're crude,
And incredibly... impolite.
They're foolish and cruel,
And they think they look... fashionable.
They destroy and they fight,
And always think they're... correct.
And that's what's wrong with HUUUUMANS!

There was an awkward silence as Uncle Fernando took a bow before flying back down. Aunt Maria gave him an embarrassed clap.

"You know," said Min thoughtfully, "if you changed a few of those words, you could make it rhyme."

Uncle Fernando's face turned bright red with anger. "And they're obsessed with rhymes!" he shouted. "If I wanted criticism,

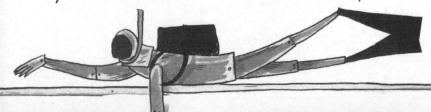

I would have asked for it. Pan, get over here. We're leaving."

"Already?" I said.

The four of us looked at each other in horror.

"But you just got here!" said Jayden.

"Yes, and it's already been too long," said Aunt Maria, turning up her snout. She undid the straps on Uncle Fernando's backpack and removed a folded-up wetsuit and another small glass helmet. She tossed them to Pan. "Your uncle made you this diving helmet for going underwater. Not that we're expecting any gratitude from you. Go on, put it on."

"I'm not getting in the toilet," said Pan.

"Oh, yes, you are, sunshine," said Uncle Fernando as he and Aunt Maria started putting their wetsuits back on.

"Just be grateful that we're not making

you fly once we reach the ocean," said Aunt Maria. "Your poor uncle is going to have to carry you to Mexico. And him with his back."

Uncle Fernando flexed his flabby arms. "Lucky for you, Pan, I've still got these bad boys. You don't get this sort of strength from prawn crackers, trust me."

"You can't go yet!" I said.

Uncle Fernando placed his hands on his hips. "Oh? And why is that?"

It was a good question, and one I didn't have an answer for. My mind scrambled for a solution but drew a blank. As everyone waited for me to speak, I glanced down at Pan, who gave me a wink before tossing the glass helmet into the air. It came as high as my chin before plummeting back to the ground.

SMASH!

All heads turned toward Pan, the helmet at his feet, smashed to pieces.

"Whoops," said Pan.

CHAPTER 7

GETTING TO KNOW YOU

"You did that on purpose!" shouted Uncle Fernando.

"No, I didn't," said Pan. "It just slipped." He was trying his best to look convincing, but I don't think anyone believed him.

"Can it be fixed?" asked Aunt Maria.

Uncle Fernando considered the shattered pieces of glass on the floor, examining a couple of pieces in his hands. "Some careful fire breathing should do the trick. But it'll take some time. We'll need to stay the night."

Aunt Maria looked repulsed. "US?" she

cried. "Staying with HUMANS? Don't you remember your own song? Can't we go somewhere else and come back when it's fixed?"

"Yes!" said Pan. "That sounds like a great idea."

"I'm not exactly thrilled with the situation myself, Maria," said Uncle Fernando, ignoring Pan, "but that Mini-Dragon needs to be watched. You know he smashed that helmet on purpose. He has no respect—and who do you think he got that from?"

Aunt Maria gave Min, Jayden, and me a dirty look.

"Exactly," said Uncle Fernando. "So I'm not leaving him unsupervised with the humans. We'll stay here tonight, I'll get the helmet fixed, and then we'll leave first thing in the morning."

Aunt Maria folded her arms, pouting.

"Fine," she mumbled.

As happy as I was that Pan wasn't going anywhere, for the night at least, the thought of sharing my bedroom with another two Mini-Dragons didn't exactly fill me with joy. For starters, I was running out of drawers.

Uncle Fernando carefully placed the broken pieces into his backpack, then after hastily cleaning up the bathroom with a couple of towels, I managed to get everyone back into my room. It wasn't long before Pan's uncle had taken to my desk as if it were a stage. As he told us all about their trip from Mexico to Spain to the United States in excruciating detail, Min and Jayden conveniently remembered they had to go home. Aunt Maria sat on the end of the desk chair, filing her claws. She mostly ignored her husband but occasionally piped up when he got some of the story wrong. Pan and I, meanwhile, lay on my bed. Pan had already drifted off, and I was beginning to feel my own eyes getting heavy when we heard a noise.

DIIIIIIIIIING-DONGGGGG!

"What's a 'ding-dong'?" asked Aunt Maria.

Pan let out a yawn before shaking his head. "That's the doorbell," he said. "It tells you that there's someone at the door."

"It'll be Toby looking for his dinner," I said to Pan. "Can you keep an eye on them, make sure they don't do ... well, anything really?"

"I doubt it," sighed Pan, "but I'll try."

To give you an idea of how bad it was being in the company of Pan's aunt and uncle, I had never been so happy to see Toby in all my life.

"Toby!" I said, greeting him at the front door. "It's great to see you."

"What? No, it isn't," said Toby, barging past me.

"Yes, it is," I said. "Come on in! I think Mom made hot dogs tonight."

Toby hung up his coat and then grunted something that sounded like approval as we entered the kitchen.

"Mom, Dad, look who's here," I said cheerfully.

My parents looked at me, then each other. "Everything okay, Eric?" asked Dad.

"Fine, thanks," I said. "Just happy Toby's here, that's all."

Mom put her hand on my forehead. "Hmm … he doesn't have a fever," she said. "You sure you're not sick? Do you want to go upstairs and lie down?"

"No!" I blurted out. Going back upstairs was the last thing I wanted to do. "Honestly, I'm fine."

SNAP!

"Now, Posy, no camera at the table," said Mom, taking the device from her. Posy, strapped into her high chair, reacted exactly how you would expect a two-and-a-half-year-old to react to having their favorite toy taken away—she cried. A lot.

"Oh, dear," said Dad. "She loves that thing."

"Mom got me one of those," said Toby as he dug into a hot dog. It'd take more than a screaming toddler to distract Toby from his food. "A little more advanced than

Posy's, obviously. It's top-of-the-line—just like the pros use. *Really* expensive."

For some reason, it quickly came back to me how annoying Toby was.

I normally hated playing video games with Toby. I always had to lose, or else he'd find a way to get me in trouble. But tonight, I was just glad I didn't have to go back upstairs for a while. Still, I couldn't help feeling guilty for leaving Pan to deal with his aunt and uncle by himself.

Once Toby had left, it was time to face the music, and I made my way up the stairs. But when I got to my room, I found Pan by himself, reading comics and chomping away on some prawn crackers. In a period of just a few seconds, I went through five distinct stages:

1. Relief — phew! They weren't here.

2. Hope — Maybe they'd changed their minds and gone home without Pan.

3. Doubt — That didn't seem likely....

4. Sadness — No, there was no chance that was what had happened.

5. Fear — So where were they, and what were they up to?

"They went to find something to eat," said Pan. "I told them not to leave, but they wouldn't listen."

"How hard did you try?" I asked.

"Not very," admitted Pan. "In fact, I … um…. Never mind."

I looked at Pan suspiciously. "What were you going to say?"

Pan put down the comic book. "All right…. Well, I sort of had an idea for how to get rid of them."

I could tell this wasn't going to be good. "An idea?"

"Yeah," said Pan, nodding. "I offered them some prawn crackers, but they laughed in my face. They said they needed something with meat on it. So I told them where they could find food like that. Nearby."

I thought about this for a few moments and then let out a huge gasp. "Not Patches!" I said.

"It's not as bad as it sounds," he said.

I thought about this. "Are you sure?

Because it sounds pretty bad to me. You sent your aunt and uncle to eat my cat!"

"Okay, when you put it like that, it sounds bad," said Pan. "But don't worry—my aunt and uncle are terrible hunters. Patches isn't in any trouble. I'm figuring she'll take one look at them and run them out of town."

"And if she doesn't?" I asked, not entirely sure who I was more worried about—Patches or the Mini-Dragons.

"Haven't really thought that far," admitted Pan.

"AHHHHHHHHH!" screamed a voice that was unmistakably Pan's aunt.

Pan and I looked at each other in horror, then bolted out the door.

"Eric, is everything all right?" shouted Mom from downstairs.

"Fine, Mom!" I shouted back. "I just ... stubbed my toe on my bed."

"Ouch. Okay, well, be careful."

Actually, the scream had come from Posy's bedroom. We opened the door to find a petrified Aunt Maria trembling in one corner of the room and Patches in the other.

"Where's Uncle Fernando?" I asked.

"I think those are his legs," said Pan. "Hanging out of Patches's mouth."

CHAPTER 8

THE MEXICAN STAND-OFF

It's difficult to know what to do in situations like these. Situations where your friend's uncle is being eaten by your cat.

Do you:

a) Demand the cat release the uncle (which could backfire—cats are not reasonable creatures and don't like to negotiate).

b) Wrestle the cat to the ground and extract the uncle from its jaws. (This will almost surely result in you walking away with a million scratches—if you walk away at all, that is.)

I had to admit c) did have a certain appeal. If Uncle Fernando escaped, then great, I guess. But if he didn't, then ... Pan would have to stay! No way could Aunt Maria carry him back to Mexico. Wait—how on earth could I think that? What kind of monster was I?

"Help him!" screamed Aunt Maria.

I made a move toward Patches, but Pan shot ahead of me until he was about a foot away from the greedy feline.

"Patches," he said in a low voice. "I want you to release my uncle. We can do this the easy way or the hard way."

Patches stared at Pan, unblinking. Uncle Fernando's legs wriggled helplessly, which at least confirmed he was still alive. Just when it looked like Patches wasn't going to back down, Pan took a deep breath and released a huge burst of flame that came within inches of the cat's face—and Uncle Fernando's legs.

Now, Patches didn't like a lot of things including, but not limited to:

- People
- Cheap cat food
- Anyone sitting in her favorite spot on the couch
- Dogs
- Other cats
- The vet (see "People")
- Baths
- Brushes
- Being fried to a crisp by Mini-Dragons

Of all the things Patches hates, that last one is probably the most important one here. She spat out Uncle Fernando, sending him skidding across the room in a trail of saliva, before bolting out of the room, almost knocking over Posy, who was standing in the hall. Seeing her, I quickly closed the door and made a mental note to check her camera later.

"Fernando!" wailed Aunt Maria, flinging herself into his arms, only to realize that she, too, was now covered in cat saliva. **"Ugggggghhhhhh!"** she cried, shoving him away.

"Just so everyone's clear," I said, looking directly at Pan, who was avoiding my gaze. "There will be no more hunting of my cat."

"Maybe if you'd put out a decent spread for your guests, instead of prawn crackers, they wouldn't have been forced to find their own food," said Aunt Maria.

"It looked to me like the only one finding

food was Patches," I said. "It wouldn't kill you to thank Pan, by the way. He did just save your life."

"He's the one who told us where to find the cat," said Uncle Fernando. "He didn't say anything about it being a ruthless killing machine. Although obviously I had the situation under control. Two more seconds and I would have toasted the big furball."

I rolled my eyes.

"Come on, Uncle Fernando," sighed Pan. "Let's get you cleaned up."

"That's the first sensible thing you've said since we got here," he replied.

Pan led his relatives to the bathroom. When we got there, Pan and I watched them with curiosity. They weren't heading toward the sink. They weren't even heading toward the bathtub or the shower.

I looked at Pan. "They're not...?" I said.

They were.

PLONK!

PLONK!

They were in the toilet. *Again.*

"Ah, the water's perfect," said Uncle Fernando.

"It's the only decent thing in this place," agreed Aunt Maria.

"I thought dragons hated water," I said, remembering a note from the *Encyclopaedia Dragonica*.

"We're washing ourselves," came Uncle Fernando's voice from the toilet bowl. "Not drinking it—that would be disgusting."

"Yeah, *that* would be disgusting," said Pan sarcastically.

I frowned. There was water all over the floor. "I just cleaned this place," I sighed, grabbing another towel.

"A little manual labor never hurt anyone," said Uncle Fernando. "They'll be plenty of that waiting for you back in Mexico, Pan. We'll build some character in you yet, mark my words."

A gloomy-looking Pan slumped to the floor. It was going to be horrible not having Pan around, but I realized that it would be much worse for him having to live with those two. I wished I could just make our problems disappear.

Then I realized I could. My eyes had drifted to the toilet handle.

It would be so easy.

I could literally flush our problems away.

So easy....

No, I thought. It wouldn't work. True enough, they didn't have their wetsuits, but I had no doubt they'd still manage to get back somehow.

Still ... we might get a couple of hours without them, which would be nice.

No, it was a crazy idea. There's no way I could do it.

"Hey, how about some soap down here?" shouted Uncle Fernando.

FLUSH!!!

I stood there for a few moments in stunned silence. Slowly I turned my head toward the toilet handle where Pan now dangled from it, a look of regret on his face.

"I'm sorry," he said. "Did you want to do that?"

When Pan's aunt and uncle eventually
showed up again, they were not happy.

Obviously.

My bedroom door opened and the two of
them stepped in, soaked from head to tail,
and fuming. Pan and I tried our best not to
laugh, but it was tough.

"You flushed us down the toilet!" said
Aunt Maria, pointing a claw at Pan.

"While we were bathing, I might add,"
said Uncle Fernando, as if that somehow
made it worse.

"Did he put you up to it?" asked Aunt
Maria, pointing toward me.

"No," snapped Pan. "I did it myself,
because I don't want you here. And I don't
want to live with you. I want to stay with Eric."

"Mini-Dragons don't belong with humans!"

shouted Uncle Fernando. "You're coming
home with us, and that's the end of it." He
snatched the washcloth I had offered them.
After drying himself, he took a bite out of the
material.

Aunt Maria looked appalled. "Fernando!
Junk food!"

"I'm starving, Maria!" he said. "I haven't
had a goat in days, and in the last few
hours I've been almost eaten by a cat and
flushed down the toilet. Would you rather I
ate a prawn cracker?"

For the rest of the night, the atmosphere
in my room was tense, to say the least.
Uncle Fernando worked alone on the top of
my chest of drawers, repairing the broken
helmet by fusing the pieces back together
with his dragon breath. Pan sulked in his sock
drawer. I pretended I had some homework to
do, and Aunt Maria went to bed early.

My bed.

Uncle Fernando and Aunt Maria refused to sleep in my drawers and, with the mood they were in, I didn't feel like arguing with them.

So, at bedtime I took a spare blanket and pillow out of the linen closet, lay down on the floor, and fell asleep.

It was early the following morning when I woke up, thanks to a tiny claw pressing into my cheek.

"Pan?" I yawned. "What do you want?"

"Shhh!" he whispered. He pointed toward my bed, where I could hear the sound of two Mini-Dragons snoring. "I think I have a plan to get rid of them for good."

I rubbed my eyes, still half asleep. "Pan, you've already tried feeding them to my cat and flushing them down the toilet. What else can you possibly come up with?"

Pan whispered in my ear.

I sat bolt upright, completely awake.

I didn't think it was possible, but Pan had come up with an idea that made the others seem harmless.

It was terrifying.

It was crossing a line.

It might just work.

CHAPTER 9
AN UNEXPECTED GIFT

Toby's mom answered the door wearing a fluffy pink robe, and her normally neat hair looking like a lion's mane, shooting off in all directions. But some things never change—she was still tapping away on her phone, barely acknowledging me.

"Is Toby here?" I asked.

Her eyes drifted briefly from the screen to me and then back again.

She walked off without saying a word.
Moments later, a bleary-eyed Toby
appeared wearing what I knew was a very
expensive pair of silk pajamas. I knew
because like with all of his things, he made
sure I knew what they cost.

"Crispo?" he said. "Do you know what
time it is?"

"Sorry, I know it's early," I said.

"What do you want?" yawned Toby.

"Here," I said, shoving a taped-up
shoebox into his hands.

"What's this?" he asked.

"It's something you've wanted forever," I
said.

Toby's eyes lit up. "A Ferrari?"

"What? No!" I said, shaking my head.
"How would I even…. No—the *other* thing
you've wanted forever."

Toby had to think for a moment or two.

"You don't mean…? Not the dragon toy?"

I nodded. "Yes. Well, no, not that one. But one just like it. Two, in fact."

Toby suddenly didn't seem so tired anymore. In fact, I couldn't remember seeing him more alert. "*Two* dragon toys?" he said. "Just like that?"

"Just like that," I said.

Toby went to open the box, but I put my hand on his. "No," I said firmly. "Not here. Wait until you're inside."

Toby looked at me suspiciously. "What's going on? Why would you give these to me? Where did you even get them? I can't find them anywhere."

"Enough questions," I said. "Do you want them or not?"

Toby looked at the box. "Well, yeah, of course, but—"

"Great," I said. "Enjoy!"

I turned and ran back toward my house, leaving before Toby could utter another word.

Pan and I sat on the end of my bed, contemplating what we had just done.

"Min and Jayden are coming over this morning," I said, trying to break the silence.

"Oh?" said Pan quietly. "That'll be nice. Do you think we should have told my aunt and uncle that Toby thinks we're all toys? To avoid confusion, I mean?"

I thought about this, then shook my head. "No," I said. "We would have had to wake them up first for that. And they wouldn't have listened anyway."

Pan nodded, and we returned to sitting in silence.

"We're horrible, aren't we?" I said,

after a while.

Pan nodded. "A little bit," he said. "But not as horrible as they are."

"We just gave your horrible aunt and uncle to the most horrible person we know. That makes us horrible times horrible."

"We're horrible squared?" asked Pan.

"I think so," I said.

A picture formed in my head of Toby playing with the Mini-Dragons. What if he wanted them to light their own farts like he had seen Pan do once? Somehow I couldn't picture Aunt Maria agreeing to that. But Toby doesn't like to take no for an answer. I imagined him tearing the two of them apart, looking for the buttons that made them breathe fire.

I knew what we had to do.

"We have to get them back," I said, with zero enthusiasm.

Pan let out a resigned groan. "You're right. We can't just leave them with Toby. No one deserves that."

It was going to be easier said than done, though. Toby had wanted a Mini-Dragon "toy" forever—he wasn't going to hand them over without a fight.

There was a knock at the door. Pan and I looked at each other.

A few moments later, Dad shouted up the stairs. "Eric, Toby's here!"

Downstairs, I found a very agitated and jittery Toby waiting for me. Before I could open my mouth, he had shoved the shoebox back into my hands.

Then he ran away.

"Well, that can't be good," I said to myself. I hated to imagine what could have happened for Toby to give them up so easily.

116

I brought the box back up to my room and then opened the lid. Two very angry Mini-Dragons glared back at me.

"Oh, there you are!" I said, hoping to sound relieved that we had found them.

"Don't either of you even try to talk your way out of this one," said Uncle Fernando

as they both flew out of the box and
perched themselves on my dresser.

"What did you do to Toby?" I asked.

"Toby?" said Uncle Fernando. "Is that
what you call him? The silly boy seemed to
think we were toys. Kept putting us up on his
shelf. So I tried giving him a history lesson on
Mini-Dragons, but then he started yammering
on about finding my 'Off' switch until
eventually he bundles us back into the box. A
very rude young man, but no more than I've
come to expect from humans."

"You're in for it now," said Aunt Maria,
shaking a claw at Pan.

Pan didn't seem to care. "Oh, yeah? It's
not like you could do anything worse to me
than make me go and live with you."

"I wouldn't be so sure about that," said
Uncle Fernando. "There's still one thing we
can do that you'll dislike even more."

"And what's that?" asked Pan, folding his arms.

Aunt Maria gave her nephew a cruel smirk before saying, "We're going to tell your mom on you!"

CHAPTER 10

FAMILY REUNION

"Eric, your friends are here!" shouted Mom.

"Thanks, Mom," I said, rushing down the stairs to greet Min and Jayden. "Can we keep using the computer?"

"Okay," she replied. "But remember, I'll need it in a little while for my class."

At the top of the stairs, Min and Jayden looked at me with concern. "Everything all right, Eric?" asked Jayden.

"No," I said, before filling them in on our attempts to get rid of the unwelcome Mini-Dragons.

"Wow," said Min. "You really handed them over to Toby?"

I nodded. "Although it's probably Toby we should feel sorry for."

"Where are they now?" asked Jayden.

"They're in the computer room speaking to Pan's parents," I said. "Getting him into trouble. But I have an idea."

Min frowned. "It doesn't sound like your ideas have been that great recently."

"I know," I said. "But this is our last shot. The helmet is fixed, so Fernando and Maria want to take Pan away this morning. We have to convince Pan's parents to let him stay."

The three Mini-Dragons were gathered around the laptop screen, furiously shouting over each other, as Pan's parents looked on with weary expressions. It was impossible to figure out what anyone was saying,

especially since they were all talking in their
dragon language.

"QUIET!" Pan's mom shouted at last, silencing the room. I guessed from the way she was looking at us that the switch to English was for our benefit. Whatever she had to say, she wanted everyone to hear it. She reminded me of my own mom in a lot of ways. She was kindhearted, but there was definitely a side of her that you didn't want to mess with.

"Pan," she said in a much lower voice, "I'm very disappointed in you. Your behavior is unacceptable. First you smash your diving helmet, which I don't believe for a second was an accident. Then you send your uncle off to hunt a cat … when you know perfectly well your uncle is a hopeless hunter."

"Hey!" protested Uncle Fernando.

"Then you flush them down the toilet," continued Mrs. Long, ignoring Fernando.

"And *then* you bundle them into a box and give them away!"

"We didn't raise you to behave like that, did we?" said Pan's dad.

Pan shook his head.

"He'd better not behave like this when he's living with us," said Aunt Maria.

"I don't want to live with you!" shouted Pan.

"Now, son," said Pan's dad, "we've been over this. Until it's safe for you to return to China, you have to live with your aunt and uncle. Only other Mini-Dragons can teach you the ancient Mini-Dragon ways."

Pan didn't look convinced. "Ancient Mini-Dragon ways?" he said. "Like the dragon codes that only dragons know how to use?"

"Exactly," said Pan's dad.

"That Eric managed to figure out in, like, five seconds?" said Pan.

His father squirmed a little. "Well … all right, so he got lucky there. But only a Mini-Dragon can bestow upon another Mini-Dragon the five qualities they must have if they're to become well-rounded adults. Leadership, Ingenuity, Bravery, Loyalty, and Kindness."

Pan's aunt and uncle nodded smugly in agreement, not that I had seen them display any of those qualities themselves.

"But Pan already has all of these things," I said.

"Oh, yes," said Aunt Maria, smirking. "He was very kind when he flushed us down the toilet. And *so* loyal when he gave us away. How brave he was sending us off to get eaten! What ingenuity he showed when smashing his helmet! And he displays such tremendous leadership letting himself be brainwashed by a human!"

The room fell silent. Everyone was looking at me for a response. I could feel my blood boiling. There had to be a way to prove them wrong.

"I'll be right back," I said, rushing out the door.

I found Posy downstairs looking at a book with Dad. She caught sight of me, smiled, and then raised her little camera and almost blinded me with the flash.

"Thought I'd take Posy through some of the photo albums," said Dad. "As it looks like we've got a little photographer on our hands here."

"Hey, Posy," I said. "Would it be okay if I borrowed your camera for a bit?"

"Oh-kay," she said, handing it to me.

Out of curiosity, I picked up the photo album and quickly thumbed through it. "Actually, can I borrow this, too?" I asked.

"Sure," said Dad, giving me an odd look. "What for, exactly?"

"Just a little project I'm working on!" I shouted as I raced up the stairs.

CHAPTER 11
THE CASE FOR PAN TO STAY

I burst into the room, put down the photo
album, and started scrolling through the
hundreds of pictures Posy had taken on
the camera. As I got to the end, I almost
fell over. What I had been looking for was
there, but there was also something even
better.

"Eric, is everything all right?" asked Pan.

"The boy has completely lost it," muttered
Uncle Fernando.

"No, I haven't," I said, "and everything's
fine. Better than fine." I plugged the camera

into the laptop and started clicking away.

"Okay," I said at last, looking directly at Pan's parents on the screen. "You want leadership? Take a look at this."

I attached the files and clicked the send button on the computer. It made a little whooshing noise as it sent a bunch of images to Pan's parents. I watched as they opened the e-mail on screen.

"I don't understand," said Pan's mom. "What am I looking at?"

I double-clicked on the files so that everyone could see the pictures. Images of a party appeared on the screen. "These," I said, "are photographs taken from my parents' surprise party. A party that Pan organized every last detail of—from the invitations to the decorations to the music to the color of the balloons. He arranged it all. How's that for leadership?"

Pan's parents looked impressed. "You did all that?" asked his father.

Pan nodded.

"That woman in the photos reminds me of someone," said Mrs. Long before shaking her head. "Well, I mean, it's very impressive, but still—"

"I'm not finished," I interrupted. "There's more. I'm sending you a video file."

I couldn't believe it was on there. Posy had been hanging around outside the room when it happened, and she must have been filming at the same time. I opened the file. The footage was pretty shaky—probably about as good as you could expect from a two-and-a-half-year-old who had accidentally switched the camera on to video mode—but it was good enough to show the moment when Pan confronted Patches and saved his uncle's life.

Pan's parents let out huge gasps.

"My little boy!" said his mom, holding her claws over her mouth. "So brave!"

"Good job, son!" said his dad, beaming with pride.

An indignant Uncle Fernando sniffed. "I had a perfectly good plan for escaping," he said.

"Was your plan to let Patches choke on you?" asked Jayden, causing everyone to burst out laughing. Except Pan's aunt and uncle, of course.

Min must have figured out what I was trying to do, as she was already flicking through the photo album. Her face lit up as she removed a photo and held it up to the screen. It was a picture of my dad and the soccer team he managed, the Kickers, celebrating on the pitch.

"Here's loyalty," she said, her face beaming with pride. "This is a picture of Eric's dad's soccer team after winning their second game in history—thanks to Pan, who stayed up all night working on their game plan after he accidentally set them on fire and got Eric into a ton of trouble."

There was a brief silence as it seemed to dawn on Min that the last part of that story didn't make Pan sound so good.

"Moving on," said Jayden quickly, who was also holding a photo. He held it up to the screen. It was a picture taken from my ninth birthday party, with Toby shooting through the air on my electric scooter. "Ingenuity," said Jayden. "Pan once made a scooter fly."

Of course, Jayden had left out the part about Pan doing this by accident. And the part where the scooter crashed into a tree moments later.

Pan's dad had an excited look on his face. "I had no idea you were into tinkering," he said, looking admiringly at Pan. "Chip off the old claw, eh? Have you done anything else?"

"Well, I once made a golf cart go faster than a car," admitted Pan.

"Wow!" said his father. "That's

amazing. You must tell me all about it sometime."

"I will," said a grinning Pan.

It looked like we were starting to win over Mr. Long, but I wasn't so sure about his wife. She looked delighted to hear good things about her son, but she had that same pained look on her face that my mom got when it was time to break it to me that I had to go to the dentist.

So I looked directly at her.

"Pan is the kindest person or Mini-Dragon I know, Mrs. Long," I said. "These things he's done, they were all to help others. You don't have to worry about him learning those Mini-Dragon qualities. He already has them."

Everyone was looking at me in amazement. There was complete silence.

"I've never heard such garbage in all my life," said Aunt Maria.

"Oh, put a sock in it, Maria," said Pan's dad. "Can't you see what's happened here?"

If she did, she was too outraged to say.

"At some point in their life, every Mini-Dragon will seek out a companion," said Mr. Long in a solemn voice. "The bond that forms between them will last a lifetime. Of course, the companion is almost always another Mini-Dragon, but it has been known for it to be a human. It happened to my own brother, actually. He became friends with a man—a mountain climber who stumbled across his cave one day. They ended up writing a book together, all about dragons. It was called—"

"*The Encyclopaedia Dragonica?*" interrupted Min.

"Oh, you've heard of it!" said Pan's dad, looking impressed. "Anyway, a Mini-Dragon

136

companionship is not something that should be taken lightly." He turned to his wife. "I think maybe we should reconsider...."

I was ready to start celebrating there and then, until I saw Mrs. Long's face.

"I'm sorry," she said, shaking her head. "Everything you've told me is wonderful, Eric. Pan, I'm so proud of you. And I'm very happy that you've met these wonderful people. But a Mini-Dragon's place is with other Mini-Dragons. I won't change my mind on the subject."

"But Mom—" protested Pan.

He was cut off by the sound of the door opening.

"All right, Eric, time's up," said Mom, standing in the doorway, decked out in her yoga gear.

Everyone froze. The Mini-Dragons had *actually* frozen, but Min, Jayden, and I

were glued to the spot, too. In fact, as Mom looked around the room, it felt like time itself had stopped.

Eventually, she let out a little chuckle. "What is it with you kids and dragons at the moment?" she said. She looked at Min and Jayden while pointing toward Aunt Maria and Uncle Fernando. "I presume those two are yours?"

Min and Jayden nodded slowly.

"And that'll be the video game, no doubt," she said, pointing toward the laptop where Mr. and Mrs. Long stared, motionless, from the screen. "Anyway, wrap things up, Eric. I'll be starting my class soon."

"Yes, Mom," I said, my voice barely a whisper.

When the door closed behind us, I almost fell over in relief.

"That was close," said Jayden.

"Pan can stay," a voice muttered.

"Yeah, I know," I said to Jayden.

"I thought Mom was definitely about to....
Wait, what was that?"

All heads turned toward the screen.

"Pan can stay," repeated Mrs. Long.

"He can?" said her husband, looking as
shocked as everyone else.

"Don't you know who that was?" she said
as she fanned her face with her tiny claws.
"That was the yoga woman! Pan's staying
with the yoga woman!"

"The one from the internet?" asked Pan's
dad.

Mrs. Long nodded, giddy with excitement. "My son is staying with the famous yoga lady. Wait until I tell all my friends!" She looked at me. "Can you get her autograph for me, Eric?"

"No problem," I laughed.

I couldn't believe it. Pan was staying. I had never felt so happy in all my life. I looked around to find him.

He wasn't there.

Neither were his aunt and uncle.

CHAPTER 12

DOWN WE GO

"Hold it right there!" I said, bursting into the bathroom. Instinctively, I knew that's where they would be. Pan's aunt and uncle were perched on the edge of the toilet with Pan trapped underneath Uncle Fernando's right arm. He was wriggling furiously, trying to escape, but his uncle was much too strong for him. The three of them were already dressed in their wetsuits. Aunt Maria slammed the glass helmet onto Pan's head.

"Adios, humans," said Uncle Fernando, giving us all a farewell salute.

"Don't you dare!" shouted Pan's mom as Jayden and Min arrived behind me, Jayden carrying the laptop in his arms.

"Honestly, Isabel, you're not thinking straight," said Aunt Maria. "Letting your son stay with a human? It's preposterous! No, you'll come to thank us for this, trust me. It's for the best."

"Leave him, Maria," demanded Pan's dad. "Or so help me, we'll come and get him from you ourselves."

Uncle Fernando let out a dismissive chuckle. "Good luck with that, Cheng," he said. "Mexico is huge, and we don't stay in the same spot for very long. Actually, maybe we won't even go back to Mexico. Wherever we go, you'll never find us. We'll be sure to send you a postcard from time to time, though."

A desperate Pan managed to wriggle his arms free and flung the helmet to the floor, smashing it to pieces once again. Min, Jayden, and I let out a cheer, but our celebration was short-lived.

"Thought you might try that," said Aunt Maria. "You can wear this instead." She strapped a tiny scuba mask onto Pan's head—it was the one from my Scuba Dave bath toy.

"Don't worry about Pan," laughed Uncle Fernando. "He'll be much better off with us. Now, as the British like to say: Cheerio!"

And with that, Aunt Maria and Uncle Fernando dived into the toilet, dragging Pan along behind them.

"Pan!" cried Min.

"No!" shouted Jayden.

"My boy!" gasped Pan's dad.

I turned toward the screen. Pan's mom had a steely look in her eyes.

"Do something," she said.

It wasn't a plea. It was an order. And once again, I got the distinct impression that when Mrs. Long told you to do something, you did it.

She really was a lot like my own mom.

I ran over to the toilet, unsure what my next move was going to be. I thought about jumping in after them but decided against it because it was:

> a) Disgusting
>
> b) Pointless, since I wouldn't fit
>
> c) Disgusting

Then I saw the plunger.

I grabbed the handle, shoved it into the toilet bowl, and began pumping as if my life depended on it. Then, after about a minute...

...nothing happened.

I kept going.

"Eric," said Min after a while, laying a hand on my shoulder. "I think they're gone."

"No," I said. If I stopped, I knew I'd definitely never see Pan again.

"Come on, buddy," said Jayden. "You've done all you can."

"No," I repeated.

"It's okay, Eric," said Pan's dad quietly. "You gave it your best shot. Pan's lucky to have a friend like you."

"I'm. Not. Stopping." I said. "Not. Now. Not. Ev—"

Before I could finish, I was sent flying backward as a stream of water shot out of the toilet, followed by the sound of one ... two ... three solid objects splashing back into the toilet.

"Pan!" I cried, throwing aside the plunger and fishing him out.

"Eric!" said Pan, tossing his mask back into the toilet bowl. "You saved me."

"What are you thinking!" shouted a livid Uncle Fernando.

"You're making a big mistake!" screamed Aunt Maria.

"The only mistake," said Pan's mom, "was thinking it was a good idea for you two to take care of our son. I think it's time you were on your way."

"Here, let me get the door for you," I added, reaching for the toilet handle.

FLUSH!!!

I looked at Pan, perched on my shoulder, still dripping wet, his mouth hanging wide open.

"I'm sorry," I said. "Did you want to do that?"

A couple of days later, and things were back to normal. Well, as normal as life with a Mini-Dragon can ever be. Which is not very normal. It was great to have Pan back and know that he wasn't going anywhere. It was even better to have Pan's aunt and uncle gone.

Min, Jayden, Pan, and I had arranged to meet up later that morning, but before that, I had an appointment to keep. Mr. and Mrs. Long had asked to speak to me. Alone.

"Hi, Eric," said Pan's dad. "We just want to thank you again."

"No problem, Mr. Long," I said. "I'd do anything for Pan."

Pan's parents smiled. "We're glad to hear you say that," said his mother.

"Oh? Why's that?" I asked.

"Well," she said, "since Pan won't be staying with his aunt and uncle, there's the matter of his education to address."

I shifted a little uncomfortably. "You mean Pan ... in school?" I said nervously. "We sort of tried that once before and it didn't end very well...."

"No," said Pan's dad, "not school. But there are certain things a dragon must learn."

"And as Pan's companion," continued his mom, "it's *your* job to make sure he learns them."

"It is?" I asked.

"*It is*," said Pan's parents firmly.

"Don't look so worried," said Pan's dad. "There's not a lot to it. I'm e-mailing you a file with all the information you'll need. It's only ten thousand words or so."

I almost fell off my chair.

"T-t-ten thousand words?" I stammered.

"Or so," said Mr. Long.

"Well, I suppose we'd better leave you to it," said Pan's mom. "No time like the present!"

Hang on—they wanted me to start now?

"It's school vacation!" I said.

"Wonderful!" said Mrs. Long. "So you'll have plenty of free time to devote to Pan's studies. We'll be expecting regular updates on his progress. Anyway, we'll be going now. Oh, any word on that other thing I asked you about?"

I frowned. "Yes, I sent you the autograph," I sighed, cringing at the memory of having to ask Mom for it, telling her it was for me—she thought I'd gone crazy.

I said good-bye to Pan's parents and then opened up the file they had sent. The list of tasks was endless. The first page alone said:

- Learn a dozen languages
- Invent your own language
- Read (and perform) all of Shakespeare's plays
- See the world
- Master the art of flame-cooking
- Learn to fly

I did a double-take when I read the last one. Pan had once shown me how good a flyer he is shortly after we had met. He flew like a rock, trashing my room in the process. The list of things I'd rather do than teach Pan how to fly included:

- Teach Toby how to share
- Teach Mom how to sing
- Teach Patches not to be evil
- Teach Dad how to successfully manage a soccer team

Even flushing my head down the toilet
sounded better.

In fact....

"You finished?" said Pan as I walked past
my room. "What did my parents want? Hey,
where are you going?"

I didn't reply as I walked into the
bathroom.

"Eric?" said Pan, sounding concerned.
"Eric? ERIC?"

FLUSH!!!

| SEND | SAVE | DISCARD |

FROM: Eric Crisp

TO: THELONGS_83@DRAGONNET.CN

SUBJECT: Thank you!

TRANSLATED FROM DRAGON

Hi Mom and Dad,

Just a quick note to say thanks for letting me stay with Eric. He's such a great friend. And so funny! He's always coming up with hilarious jokes. Earlier, he had this good one. He said—wait until you hear this—that you guys had given him homework for me to do! LOL! Told you he was a laugh!

Actually, it was a joke wasn't

ABOUT THE AUTHOR

Tom Nicoll has been writing since he was in school, where he enjoyed trying to fit in as much silliness in his essays as he could possibly get away with. When not writing, he enjoys playing video games (especially the ones where he gets beaten by kids half his age from all over the world). He is also a big comedy, TV, and movie nerd. Tom lives just outside Edinburgh, Scotland, with his wife and two daughters.

THERE's A DRAGON IN MY TOILET!
is his third book for children.

ABOUT THE ILLUSTRATOR

Sarah Horne grew up in Derbyshire, England, and spent much of her childhood scampering in the nearby fields with a few goats. An illustrator for more than 15 years, she started her illustration career working freelance for newspapers and magazines. When not at her desk, Sarah loves running, painting, photography, cooking, movies, and a good stomp up a hill.

She can currently be found giggling under some paper in her London studio.

PULL MY FINGER...

...PAAARP!

THERE'S A
DRAGON
IN MY
DINNER!

BY TOM NICOLL   ILLUSTRATED BY SARAH HORNE

BuuRRRP!

THERE'S A
DRAGON
IN MY
BACKPACK!

I ♥ DRAGONS

...RnnP!

BY TOM NICOLL
ILLUSTRATED BY SARAH HORNE

THERE'S A
DRAGON
IN MY
TOILET!

FLUSH...

PLOP!

BY TOM NICOLL   ILLUSTRATED BY SARAH HORNE

THERE'S A
DRAGON
IN MY
BOOT!

EEEWW!

PONG!

by TOM NICOLL
Illustrated by SARAH HORNE